I0456334

JANICE

A SEXUAL ENIGMA

RICHARD LEE

Copyright © 2020 Richard Lee Publishing

All rights reserved.

ISBN: 978-0-909431-10-5

No part of the Eros Crescent series may be reproduced in any form or by any electronic or mechanical means, including information storage and retrieval systems, without written permission from the author, except for the use of brief quotations in a book review.

Dedicated to a world in need of love and imagination.

*"If a little is great, and a lot is better,
then way too much is just about right!"*

- Mae West

CONTENTS

FOREWORD

The EROS CRESCENT novels take you on a journey like no other - to places you couldn't imagine - a female friendly sex club or a privately owned members-only dogging venue; the toy-boy life of a writer working on the Amalfi coast and much much more. *JANICE* and the other novellas - *JESSICA, MARIA, HELEN* and *THE CLUB* - are extracts taken from *The Fifi Code*, *Eros Crescent* and *Mount Eros*.

PREFACE

"It seems that the music teacher and the organist would wait until everyone had left at the end of choir practice, except for a half dozen or more lads who went and hung around in the churchyard.

"Then the two women would go back inside the vestry, change their clothes, putting on stockings and suspenders, high heels and short skirts, along with lots of makeup, then unlock the door and let the boys in."

"My goodness, Celia, stories like this could cause a sudden increase in the sizes of congregations across the land. Please tell me more."

– *from Eros Crescent*

JANICE

HELEN COULD NOT REMEMBER what led to this particular conversation, but this woman's story went something like this.

The woman, Celia Ashbee, had a son teaching at a private school whose friend, teaching at another private school, had a friend who told him a rude story. The friend of the friend of the friend said that one of his senior students and some other lads were in a church choir and that they had a great time each week after choir practice with two women.

Helen suddenly got very interested at this point, but tried to hide her enthusiasm, not wanting the nice lady to think ill of her.

"Did the friend of the friend of the friend say if the student described what happened, Celia?"

Celia poured more tea and selected a savoury *petit four*. Helen estimated that she was perhaps a little older than herself, a well-kept woman in her late fifties or very early sixties.

Celia continued her story, lowering her voice and looking around her as she spoke.

"It seems that the music teacher and the organist would wait until everyone had left at the end of practice, except for a half dozen or more young men who went and hung around in the churchyard.

"Then the two women would go back inside the vestry, change their clothes, putting on stockings and suspenders, high heels and short skirts, along with lots of makeup, then unlock the door and let the men in."

Helen found the story fascinating, and erotic.

"My goodness, Celia, stories like this could cause a sudden increase in the sizes of congregations across the land. Please tell me more."

Celia laughed, enjoying her new friend's sense of humour and impressed with Helen's seeming lack of shockability.

"Did he say what actually happened after the lads entered the vestry?"

Helen's new friend coloured up and Helen looked at her appreciatively. Celia, on the one hand a very proper upper middle-class woman of impeccable taste, hid a fun-loving naughty side which one would never have observed except via the subject matter of this conversation.

"He did, Helen. He did indeed. He said that in a very small anteroom there was a mattress covered with a bedspread, probably an emergency bed in case someone in the congregation suddenly took poorly.

"He said that the two women knelt on the mattress and called to the lads to come in, in pairs. Then they told them to show them what they had in their trousers. Once they were on display, each woman would put the young man's penis in her mouth and suck it; then after a while they would look up at his face and say …"

By this time, Helen was mesmerised by Celia's story and, it should be said, by the delightful Celia. Her looks, her beautiful voice, her smile, even the lines on her face spoke of intelligence and joy. Her fine clothes spoke of finer garments beneath, a satin camisole perhaps, expensive serviceable panties with just a touch of lace? And was she a woman who preferred wearing stockings or did she choose tights? And even though she was slim, would she own a corselet?

"Say it, Celia. Tell me what she said. You are committing story interruptus. Please, don't leave me hanging."

Celia burst out laughing, then put her hand over her mouth and looked around like a naughty girl.

"Suck or fuck?" she whispered.

Helen stared at Celia's sparkling eyes, bright with mirth.

"Gosh Celia, we're getting to the high notes now."

"Then, if the man replied with the 'f' word, the woman immediately does an about face, showing her rear end and, it is said, not wearing any knickers, at which point the fellow has his way.

"If he has any difficulty finding his way, and if the woman beside her is facing the front and has a moment with a free hand, she will lean across and put him in. If not, a hand will come through the legs to grab him and sort him out."

Celia stopped talking and stared at Helen. She looked flushed and excited. She was fascinated with Helen. She loved her relaxed unfazed way of seeing things.

Helen looked back at her, one could even say lovingly.

There was suddenly a hush as people prepared for a final concert piece by three young violinists.

"Celia?"

"Yes, Helen?"

"Can I write down my telephone number and give it to you? And maybe we could catch up some time soon. I love talking to you, so I hope we can see each other again."

"Please, yes. And I will call you very soon. You are great company and I do get lonely for someone to talk with who is happy to talk about anything."

"Thank you. Oh, I forgot to ask, can you tell me the name of the church or do you need to keep it a secret?"

"Ah, yes, I hadn't really thought about that. Perhaps if I just say it begins with a J, Helen."

"Hello, Helen."

Helen had walked over to the house to get a knife sharpener. She always meant to buy one for the studio but then, when shopping, she forgot.

Helen was startled by the voice. She looked up.

"Sorry Helen, if I surprised you. I came through Mary's gate and saw you leaving and that you had left the door open, so thought you would no doubt return soon."

"Janice! How nice to see you. Are you looking for Mary? I think it's her volunteer day at the Salvos' op shop."

"Sort of. But I really wanted to see you, Helen. Can I come in?"

Helen gestured towards the studio door.

"Be my guest, Janice."

Helen could not move her eyes away from the long, thin extraordinary body of Janice. Her legs and backside were almost a kinky artwork, exaggerated in a way that artists toyed with in their drawings but which quite rightly, no one ever believed depicted a real person.

But what was racing through Helen's mind at this moment was what she had said to Mary, "Be careful what you think about because it usually comes true." She had thought quite a bit about Janice since her conversation with Celia Ashbee about the goings-on at the church, and Helen was convinced that, 'J' must surely have meant St John's, and if it did, then Janice was surely one of the women entertaining the boys after choir practice.

And hadn't Mary said she thought Janice was not as innocent as she looked?

Helen steeled herself. Other than her fascination with Janice's body, she felt no special attraction to the woman. She had no thoughts about loving her and without any emotional ties it would be hard to imagine that anything would ever happen between them.

Helen closed the door and invited Janice to sit on one of the studio's three kitchen chairs.

2

LOOKING FOR LOVE

"WELL, Janice. What can I do for you? Is Mary giving you a hard time?"

Janice laughed.

"Not at all, Helen. I'm not sure how to say this, but I was always fascinated with Mary's story of your seduction of her, and how beautiful and loving it was. Over time, I've not exactly been jealous, but Mary took me quite brutally, not showing any love until later. Now whenever I think of love, I can't help thinking of you, Helen. Could we be lovers too, Helen? It would be a wonderful thing, sharing you with Mary."

Helen's mind raced as she watched an increasingly agitated Janice first lift her skirt up just above her knees and then fiddle with the buttons on her blouse, while her mouth began to gape and her tongue wandered over her lips.

Helen could thank her for her compliments and then simply ask Janice to leave. There was no way she wanted to add Janice to her list of girlfriends. And then of course there was the deceit of the woman, if she was one of the women in the story about the lads at St John's. Her story about wanting to be loved did not in any way ring true.

Helen suddenly saw what was going on. Janice was under an influence of sorts. Was it drugs? Helen guessed it was something she had first heard about many years before, when she was working in a clinic in London.

Janice was suffering from what, in the old days, was called nymphomaniac's disorder, known amongst Helen's co-workers and nurses as nympho block.

The word "nymphomaniac" was no longer in use, having been replaced with the term "hyper-sexuality", but in those days, the term "nympho block", referred to a woman who had engaged in sex contin-uously over many days, weeks or months, and who was now unable to live without it, suffering a craving like a drug addict looking for the next fix.

Of the various theories that doctors and therapists came up with, the one Helen found most plausible was the idea that these women had experienced a lot of bad sex or, put differently, incomplete sex, sex without orgasms.

Normally, regular sex between partners might be very satisfying, or it might not. The difference was that women who only had sex a couple of times a week, and did not experience regular orgasms, did not suffer this build-up, or if they did it was minor and could be over-come. Sadly, what was more likely to happen was that they just learnt to live with it or should one say, without it.

One solution offered by sex therapists was to teach a patient to orgasm more easily when having sex, and in the couple of cases Helen observed this did, over time, lead to a better outcome for the woman. And of course, the arrival of the electric vibrator changed things for many women.

What Helen was seeing here might well be the result of Janice having a lot of inexperienced young cocks giving her nothing but their quick ejaculations. These lads were not experienced males offering foreplay and long deep thrusting and prolonged enjoyment.

Unable to find a fix, Janice had finally ended up here as a last resort. Subconsciously, she understood the need for real love and, remembering Mary's story of her loving conversion by Helen, this was the only place where she might find answers.

Helen looked at Janice and saw that she now had her hand between her legs, her head had lolled back, and her eyes were closed.

Then she recalled an experience she'd had in London. It was her first real lesbian romance. The older woman was Louise Lazarus, the glamorous bitch secretary of the medical centre's managing director.

Helen was dazzled by Louise's stylish clothes and elegant body, and when she invited Helen to her flat for afternoon tea, one Saturday, Helen jumped at the invitation. After she had arrived and been shown around the luxury apartment, it was only an hour or less before Louise had her tongue inside Helen's mouth and a hand inside her brassiere, and it wasn't long before she was guiding the young woman's hand along Louise's stockinged leg and up to her panties, where she lovingly showed the willing novice how to put her fingers inside her crotch and inside her.

Louise had secrets that she carried from her schooldays, and over time she revealed those secrets to Helen.

Louise had been educated at one of the smaller private girls schools near the Sussex border, in Kent. The school, or rather the staff, were expected to follow the school's long traditions regarding discipline, meaning that girls were regularly thrashed.

Flagellation or "pursuing the path of penance" as it was referred to, was a regular occurrence at the school. So endemic was it that "the art" was practiced, not only by the staff on the senior girls, but the senior girls themselves who would administer it to a select few of the staff, always in secret of course.

Whippings, strappings, spankings, floggings of every description were a major topic of conversation. Everything at school rotated around who had what done to them, or what they had done to someone else.

So popular was this pastime that it would seem to have been the foremost form of entertainment for the hormonally charged scholars, and quite naturally girlfriends looked after one another, tending each other's discomfort with soothing balms and very loving words.

Thus "pursuing the path of penance" facilitated the continuation of the school's healthy lesbian traditions, endowing the nation with the strong women necessary for providing the special sort of workers and wives required to serve alongside the public school men of the aristocracy and the upper classes, and ultimately to ensure the success and safety of the empire.

Stately homes, along with the nice houses of the public servants taking the early morning trains to Westminster or the City in their bowler hats – and with extreme punctuality – were ruled by women of substance, women who knew where their responsibilities lay, along with their understanding of certain things that their husbands didn't know that they knew.

Adaptability was an essential quality for the public school educated woman, especially when she eventually took her marital vows, and shouldered the responsibilities that being a wife demanded, be they judging the flowers at the village fete or organising the house staff on an Indian tea plantation, or overseeing the affairs of the family and the estate, while her officer husband was away on some foreign battlefield.

Within days Louise had made Helen her protege, and shortly after that her sex slave, having Helen whenever, however and wherever she wanted.

From then on, Helen felt a wetness between her legs whenever Louise spoke her name, and she bent her knees just a little the moment her mistress came towards her.

The medical centre where Helen and Louise worked specialised in gynaecological problems. Woman would present with all sorts of situations, and every once in a while, if there was someone with a case of hyper-sexuality who was suffering, the powers that be would give a wink and nod, and indicate to Louise that this might be a case of "nympho block" and that she could perhaps help the sufferer.

Helen remembers returning home to Louise's house one evening after working late. Immediately she shut the front door behind her, she heard screams which she knew could only mean that someone was being flogged.

Knowing better than to disturb her mistress in full flagellator mode, Helen nonetheless, went and listened at the door of the punishment room.

Things had obviously been going on for some time. The person being flogged was well past screaming "No, please, no more" and now sang out in a high pitched wailing scream, "More, yes, yes, oh please, more." This was followed a little later by a deafening scream that seemed to go on for ages, as the woman reached her orgasm.

As Helen turned to leave, the door flew open and Louise walked out and seeing her, and with her eyes shining brightly from the excitement that she had just enjoyed, grabbed her and kissed her passionately on the lips and, pushing her against the wall and with a hand firmly placed between her legs, said "I'm going to give you an orgasm like that, darling, very soon," then she headed to the bath room.

And she did. Only days later, Louise took Helen into the room and closed the door and proceeded to introduce her to the strap. She already new that the pain would turn to pleasure, but when it did became pleasurable, Louise didn't stop. Only when Helen vented the prolonged scream which accompanied a major orgasm did her lady lover stop beating her, and instead, took her in her arms and carried her the few steps to the big bed. But she hadn't finished.

First she lightly rubbed balm on Helen's cut up bottom. Then she put on her favourite strap-on and opened her legs and shagged her, all the time telling her how beautiful she was how sexy she was and how she was going to fuck her forever and a day.

Once a week, after work, Louise would tell Helen to put on her old school skirt and the long school socks she had saved, hidden in a drawer. Then she would make her lie back on the bed while she lifted her legs, staring at her while she ran her hand up her schoolgirl sock to the bare top of her leg, all the while touching herself with her other hand.

Then Louise would give her an evening of love-making. And when she had given her an orgasm, she would look down at her with her beautiful smile and say, "You've been such a good girl all week Helen, Miss Lazarus is going to let you have her pussy now as a reward. You can shag her just as much as you want, my child."

Then she would lift Helen up and take off her strap-on and fix it to her waist.

As Helen worked the dildo in and out of Louise's splendid pussy, and as Louise lifted up Helen's skirt and touched her legs, she stared up at her young and innocent face and spoke softly to her. "Do you love shagging your teacher, darling? Does being on top of Miss Lazarus excite you my sweet? Yes, I know it does because you are shagging Miss Lazarus so beautifully." And so Helen's introduction to love also included other people's fantasies, and she loved them.

Helen's first lady lover became her yardstick for any future relationships and she chose mostly to be a single person rather than enter into what she always sensed would be a liaison less intense than the experience the dazzling Louise had shown her.

Janice was staring at Helen with pleading eyes.

Helen looked up at objects hanging on the wall. Among the interesting miscellany of items was a well-made leather tickler, a miniature cat-o-nine-tails that Freddy had brought home as a present for her when he had been away at a convention.

She was excited when one day he picked it off the wall and laid into her bottom with it. She screamed in agony, but just as she was beginning to get a wonderful sensation that overrode the pain and would take her "all the way", Freddy stopped, believing he should not hurt his wife in this way. Helen was extremely disappointed. "That is what comes from having such a caring husband, damn it!"

The little tickler had not been taken off the wall since.

Helen was now getting hot thinking about that day with Freddy, and much further back to Louise, and the possibilities in front of her now. She could help Janice and enjoy herself at the same time.

Janice's amazing legs could not be ignored, Helen mused as she stood up and went over to her.

"Janice?"

"Yes Helen?"

"I'm going to do things to you. Okay?

"Oh yes, please Helen. Please give me some relief. If you don't, I think I will surely die. Do whatever you want to me, Helen. It must be better than dying."

"Janice?"

"Yes?"

"I'm going to whip your backside, Janice, until it turns red, and I won't let you leave until I'm finished. Are you ready for this, Janice?"

"Yes, Helen. I need to be punished for I have sinned heavily in the sight of God."

Helen knew enough about addicts. They loved to be theatrical and talk rubbish, though often it did relate to some real event in their lives.

"Would you like me to kiss you first, Janice, before I thrash you?"

"Yes, yes, give me your lips, Helen. I so want to be loved."

At first, she wanted to kiss Janice only to make it easier for her to launch herself on the wretched woman. Now Helen was going to love her properly, regardless. She could whip Janice with love, just as Louise had whipped Helen.

Helen led her to the divan beside the window

She began by kissing Janice, who cried and thrust her tongue into Helen's mouth. Helen accepted it, tentatively at first but then, deciding to let herself go all the way. She put her lips back on Janice's mouth and tongued her enthusiastically, while Janice groaned.

Then she slipped Janice's skirt down over the long legs and made her lie down on her back. Helen lifted her legs high up in the air as she did with all of her lovers, and told her not to move.

Helen grabbed a charcoal pencil and a pad and quickly sketched the magic legs and the unusual bubble backside, incongruous on such a thin body.

Then Helen slowly caressed Janice's legs and kissed the backs of her knees, and all the while Helen couldn't stop touching her own wet pussy and she smiled inwardly, knowing that this was a good sign.

Janice continued sobbing, all the time murmuring, "Yes Helen, yes Helen, please Helen." Then Helen reached for the tickler on the wall.

When Janice screamed the giant scream that accompanied her most extraordinary orgasm ever, Helen orgasmed too, and not just lightly. The excitement she felt while flogging Janice's rear end felt as though Janice was the one who had flogged Helen. It felt truly beautiful.

Suddenly two women, who until now, had been separated by many differences, were sharing feelings that were very rarely available to women other than via a flogging, be it by hand, the rod, or the tickler.

Janice was cured, at least until the next time. Her manner changed and Helen hoped that her habits would change. But that of course, would be up to Janice.

Helen never knew just what happened at the church after that, nor did she bother to ask. Nor did she enquire about what other things her new sexually hyperactive friend got up to.

But she knew that this new secret friend, Janice, would come to her with her long legs and body each time she felt a "nympho block" coming on, and together they would visit that secret heaven.

Helen bathed Janice's backside and delicately applied a healing balm. Janice lay still and quiet as though she was sleeping, but when Helen said in a very quiet and reassuring voice that Janice could come to her whenever she needed special help, she turned her head and with a serene smile murmured "Thank you, Helen."

And when Helen went on to ask Janice if she would keep their special time together a secret, Janice replied, "Only you and me, Helen, I promise." Then she looked up again and added, "and our little leather friend, hanging up there on the wall."

Helen put a hand on Janice's face and kissed her. "Just the three of us, darling, that's right."

Then Helen rolled Janice onto her back and lifted her legs so that they stood high in the air.

"Now Janice, please don't move for a moment. I just want to add the seams of your stockings to my drawing."

3

PURSUING THE PATH OF PENANCE

"WELL, Janice. What can I do for you? Is Mary giving you a hard time?"

Janice laughed.

"Not at all, Helen. I'm not sure how to say this, but I was always fascinated with Mary's story of your seduction of her, and how beautiful and loving it was. Over time, I've not exactly been jealous, but Mary took me quite brutally, not showing any love until later. Now whenever I think of love, I can't help thinking of you, Helen. Could we be lovers too, Helen? It would be a wonderful thing, sharing you with Mary."

Helen's mind raced as she watched an increasingly agitated Janice first lift her skirt up just above her knees and then fiddle with the buttons on her blouse, while her mouth began to gape and her tongue wandered over her lips.

Helen could thank her for her compliments and then simply ask Janice to leave. There was no way she wanted to add Janice to her list of girlfriends. And then of course there was the deceit of the woman, if she was one of the women in the story about the lads at St John's. Her story about wanting to be loved did not in any way ring true.

Helen suddenly saw what was going on. Janice was under an influence of sorts. Was it drugs? Helen guessed it was something she had first heard about many years before, when she was working in a clinic in London.

Janice was suffering from what, in the old days, was called nymphomaniac's disorder, known amongst Helen's co-workers and nurses as nympho block.

The word "nymphomaniac" was no longer in use, having been replaced with the term "hyper-sexuality", but in those days, the term "nympho block", referred to a woman who had engaged in sex continuously over many days, weeks or months, and who was now unable to live without it, suffering a craving like a drug addict looking for the next fix.

Of the various theories that doctors and therapists came up with, the one Helen found most plausible was the idea that these women had experienced a lot of bad sex or, put differently, incomplete sex, sex without orgasms.

Normally, regular sex between partners might be very satisfying, or it might not. The difference was that women who only had sex a couple of times a week, and did not experience regular orgasms, did not suffer this build-up, or if they did it was minor and could be overcome. Sadly, what was more likely to happen was that they just learnt to live with it or should one say, without it.

One solution offered by sex therapists was to teach a patient to orgasm more easily when having sex, and in the couple of cases Helen observed this did, over time, lead to a better outcome for the woman. And of course, the arrival of the electric vibrator changed things for many women.

What Helen was seeing here might well be the result of Janice having a lot of inexperienced young cocks giving her nothing but their quick ejaculations. These lads were not experienced males offering foreplay and long deep thrusting and prolonged enjoyment.

Unable to find a fix, Janice had finally ended up here as a last resort. Subconsciously, she understood the need for real love and, remembering Mary's story of her loving conversion by Helen, this was the only place where she might find answers.

Helen looked at Janice and saw that she now had her hand between her legs, her head had lolled back, and her eyes were closed.

Then she recalled an experience she'd had in London. It was her first real lesbian romance. The older woman was Louise Lazarus, the glamorous bitch secretary of the medical centre's managing director.

Helen was dazzled by Louise's stylish clothes and elegant body, and when she invited Helen to her flat for afternoon tea, one Saturday, Helen jumped at the invitation. After she had arrived and been shown around the luxury apartment, it was only an hour or less before Louise had her tongue inside Helen's mouth and a hand inside her brassiere, and it wasn't long before she was guiding the young woman's hand along Louise's stockinged leg and up to her panties, where she lovingly showed the willing novice how to put her fingers inside her crotch and inside her.

Louise had secrets that she carried from her schooldays, and over time she revealed those secrets to Helen.

Louise had been educated at one of the smaller private girls schools near the Sussex border, in Kent. The school, or rather the staff, were expected to follow the school's long traditions regarding discipline, meaning that girls were regularly thrashed.

Flagellation or "pursuing the path of penance" as it was referred to, was a regular occurrence at the school. So endemic was it that "the art" was practiced, not only by the staff on the senior girls, but the senior girls themselves who would administer it to a select few of the staff, always in secret of course.

Whippings, strappings, spankings, floggings of every description were a major topic of conversation. Everything at school rotated around who had what done to them, or what they had done to someone else.

So popular was this pastime that it would seem to have been the foremost form of entertainment for the hormonally charged scholars, and quite naturally girlfriends looked after one another, tending each other's discomfort with soothing balms and very loving words.

Thus "pursuing the path of penance" facilitated the continuation of the school's healthy lesbian traditions, endowing the nation with the strong women necessary for providing the special sort of workers and wives required to serve alongside the public school men of the aristocracy and the upper classes, and ultimately to ensure the success and safety of the empire.

Stately homes, along with the nice houses of the public servants taking the early morning trains to Westminster or the City in their bowler hats – and with extreme punctuality – were ruled by women of substance, women who knew where their responsibilities lay, along with their understanding of certain things that their husbands didn't know that they knew.

Adaptability was an essential quality for the public school educated woman, especially when she eventually took her marital vows, and shouldered the responsibilities that being a wife demanded, be they judging the flowers at the village fete or organising the house staff on an Indian tea plantation, or overseeing the affairs of the family and the estate, while her officer husband was away on some foreign battlefield.

Within days Louise had made Helen her protege, and shortly after that her sex slave, having Helen whenever, however and wherever she wanted.

From then on, Helen felt a wetness between her legs whenever Louise spoke her name, and she bent her knees just a little the moment her mistress came towards her.

The medical centre where Helen and Louise worked specialised in gynaecological problems. Woman would present with all sorts of situations, and every once in a while, if there was someone with a case of hyper-sexuality who was suffering, the powers that be would give a wink and nod, and indicate to Louise that this might be a case of "nympho block" and that she could perhaps help the sufferer.

Helen remembers returning home to Louise's house one evening after working late. Immediately she shut the front door behind her, she heard screams which she knew could only mean that someone was being flogged.

Knowing better than to disturb her mistress in full flagellator mode, Helen nonetheless, went and listened at the door of the punishment room.

Things had obviously been going on for some time. The person being flogged was well past screaming "No, please, no more" and now sang out in a high pitched wailing scream, "More, yes, yes, oh please, more." This was followed a little later by a deafening scream that seemed to go on for ages, as the woman reached her orgasm.

As Helen turned to leave, the door flew open and Louise walked out and seeing her, and with her eyes shining brightly from the excitement that she had just enjoyed, grabbed her and kissed her passionately on the lips and, pushing her against the wall and with a hand firmly placed between her legs, said "I'm going to give you an orgasm like that, darling, very soon," then headed to the bathroom.

And she did. Only days later, Louise took Helen into the room and closed the door and proceeded to introduce her to the strap. She already new that the pain would turn to pleasure, but when it did became pleasurable, Louise didn't stop. Only when Helen vented the prolonged scream which accompanied a major orgasm did her lady lover stop beating her, and instead, took her in her arms and carried her the few steps to the big bed. But she hadn't finished.

First she lightly rubbed balm on Helen's cut up bottom. Then she put on her favourite strap-on and opened her legs and shagged her, all the time telling her how beautiful she was how sexy she was and how she was going to fuck her forever and a day.

Once a week, after work, Louise would tell Helen to put on her old school skirt and the long school socks she had saved, hidden in a drawer. Then she would make her lie back on the bed while she lifted her legs, staring at her while she ran her hand up her schoolgirl sock to the bare top of her leg, all the while touching herself with her other hand.

Then Louise would give her her evening shag. And when she had given her an orgasm, she would look down at her with her beautiful smile and say "You've been such a good girl all week Helen, Miss Lazarus is going to let you have her pussy now as a reward. You can shag her just as much as you want, my child."

Then she would lift Helen up and take off her strap-on and fix it to her waist.

As Helen worked the dildo in and out of Louise's splendid pussy, and as Louise lifted up Helen's skirt and touched her legs, she stared up at her young and innocent face and spoke softly to her. "Do you love shagging your teacher, darling? Does being on top of Miss Lazarus excite you my sweet? Yes, I know it does because you are shagging Miss Lazarus so beautifully." And so Helen's introduction to love also included other people's fantasies, and she loved them.

Helen's first lady lover became her yardstick for any future relationships and she chose mostly to be a single person rather than enter into what she always sensed would be a liaison less intense than the experience the dazzling Louise had shown her.

Janice was staring at Helen with pleading eyes.

Helen looked up at objects hanging on the wall. Among the interesting miscellany of items was a well-made leather tickler, a miniature cat-o-nine-tails that Freddy had brought home as a present for her when he had been away at a convention.

She was excited when one day he picked it off the wall and laid into her bottom with it. She screamed in agony, but just as she was beginning to get a wonderful sensation that overrode the pain and would take her "all the way", Freddy stopped, believing he should not hurt his wife in this way. Helen was extremely disappointed. "That is what comes from having such a caring husband, damn it!"

The little tickler had not been taken off the wall since.

Helen was now getting hot thinking about that day with Freddy, and much further back to Louise, and the possibilities in front of her now. She could help Janice and enjoy herself at the same time.

Janice's amazing legs could not be ignored, Helen mused as she stood up and went over to her.

"Janice?"

"Yes Helen?"

"I'm going to do things to you. Okay?"

"Oh yes, please Helen. Please give me some relief. If you don't, I think I will surely die. Do whatever you want to me, Helen. It must be better than dying."

"Janice?"

"Yes?"

"I'm going to whip your backside, Janice, until it turns red, and I won't let you leave until I'm finished. Are you ready for this, Janice?"

"Yes, Helen. I need to be punished for I have sinned heavily in the sight of God."

Helen knew enough about addicts. They loved to be theatrical and talk rubbish, though often it did relate to some real event in their lives.

"Would you like me to kiss you first, Janice, before I thrash you?"

"Yes, yes, give me your lips, Helen. I so want to be loved."

At first, she wanted to kiss Janice only to make it easier for her to launch herself on the wretched woman. Now Helen was going to love her properly, regardless. She could whip Janice with love, just as Louise had whipped Helen.

Helen led her to the divan beside the window

She began by kissing Janice, who cried and thrust her tongue into Helen's mouth. Helen accepted it, tentatively at first but then, deciding to let herself go all the way. She put her lips back on Janice's mouth and tongued her enthusiastically, while Janice groaned.

Then she slipped Janice's skirt down over the long legs and made her lie down on her back. Helen lifted her legs high up in the air as she did with all of her lovers, and told her not to move.

Helen grabbed a charcoal pencil and a pad and quickly sketched the magic legs and the unusual bubble backside, incongruous on such a thin body.

Then Helen slowly caressed Janice's legs and kissed the backs of her knees, and all the while Helen couldn't stop touching her own wet pussy and she smiled inwardly, knowing that this was a good sign.

Janice continued sobbing, all the time murmuring, "Yes Helen, yes Helen, please Helen." Then Helen reached for the tickler on the wall.

When Janice screamed the giant scream that accompanied her most extraordinary orgasm ever, Helen orgasmed too, and not just lightly. The excitement she felt while flogging Janice's rear end felt as though Janice was the one who had flogged Helen. It felt truly beautiful.

Suddenly two women, who until now, had been separated by many differences, were sharing feelings that were very rarely available to women other than via a flogging, be it by hand, the rod, or the tickler.

Janice was cured, at least until the next time. Her manner changed and Helen hoped that her habits would change. But that of course, would be up to Janice.

Helen never knew just what happened at the church after that, nor did she bother to ask. Nor did she enquire about what other things her new sexually hyperactive friend got up to.

But she knew that this new secret friend, Janice, would come to her with her long legs and body each time she felt a "nympho block" coming on, and together they would visit that secret heaven.

Helen bathed Janice's backside and delicately applied a healing balm. Janice lay still and quiet as though she was sleeping, but when Helen said in a very quiet and reassuring voice that Janice could come to her whenever she needed special help, she turned her head and with a serene smile murmured "Thank you, Helen."

And when Helen went on to ask Janice if she would keep their special time together a secret, Janice replied, "Only you and me, Helen, I promise." Then she looked up again and added, "and our little leather friend, hanging up there on the wall."

Helen put a hand on Janice's face and kissed her. "Just the three of us, darling, that's right."

Then Helen rolled Janice onto her back and lifted her legs so that they stood high in the air.

"Now Janice, please don't move for a moment. I just want to add the seams of your stockings to my drawing."

4

JANICE BECOMES A NUN

EARLIER IN THE EVENING, during Mary's birthday party, Helen had accidentally discovered when she bent down to pick up a piece of cutlery that had dropped onto the floor, that the mother and daughter, Maria and Serina, were sitting on either side of Janice, each with a hand on one of Janice's legs, lovingly caressing her upper thighs.

Maria and Serina had just moved into Number 21, two down from Helen and Freddy's house.

Number 21 would remain empty until the new owners arrived from London in a month or two. The agent and executors of the property had employed the La Rocca family to live in the house as caretakers for however long was needed.

When Helen asked Mary about it when Mary came into the kitchen to help carry food out to the dining room, she said that they also had Maria's grandfather, Alberto living with them, and also a lodger, Giorgio, newly arrived from Italy.

When the three women were saying their goodbyes and leaving, Helen heard Serina say to Janice, "We are only two houses away, Janice. You won't have to walk far at all."

As she watched the three women head off down the driveway, she couldn't help thinking how the tall, thin Janice was like a stick insect or a praying mantis.

So why was Helen even thinking of Janice at this late hour? What mystery, if any, surrounded this woman? And in particular, what prompted these two women to put their hands on Janice's legs? And why did they leave the party early? And why were they taking Janice home to their place? She tried to put Janice out of her mind. In desperation she got up quietly, trying not to wake up Polly lying beside her, and went to the kitchen and made a cup of cocoa.

But Helen's mind wouldn't stop. Did Janice have a little-known psychological disorder? Was she able to manipulate those around her to unwittingly give her some particular kind of sexual attention? Were there different cue requirements for different sexual fantasies or desires? She had great difficulty thinking about Janice. She wished she'd never set eyes on her. Janice was an enigma. There was a mystery here that Helen might never understand.

When Janice and Maria and Serina left Mary's birthday party they held hands as they walked the few yards to the front gate of Number 21. The summer night was balmy, ideal for being outdoors.

Maria and Serina gently guided Janice along a winding path to a wide covered veranda. Instead of unlocking the door, the mother and daughter asked Janice to sit down on the comfy old sofa that sat against the wall. Then the two slowly gave in to their passions, starting by lifting Janice's legs into the air, removing her panties and taking turns in licking and sucking her cunt.

"Oh my goodness, what is happening? What are you doing to me," groaned Janice?

"Just say if you want us to stop Janice. We don't want to frighten you," Maria said quietly.

"Mum and I are hungry for you Sister Janice. Please don't worry. We won't hurt you."

But Janice loved it and lay back with just her hands fumbling in the darkness, surreptitiously seeking out the bodies of the two adoring women.

Janice smiled inside. At Mary's party, she had told Maria and Serina that she was only a week out of a convent and quite lost in this modern world. She said that she had become sexually frustrated and had fallen in love with another nun, who had rejected her and reported her to the Mother Superior.

She told Maria and Serina that she had been asked to leave. It had been suggested that she could join a teaching order and become a teacher and had been told to go away and think about it.

She finished her story by shedding a tear and dabbing her eyes and, within minutes, first Maria and then Serina put a hand on a thigh and caressed her above her stockings, whispering their desire to help her, and Janice knew she was on her way.

Maria and Serina had both been boarders at convent schools and both girls had been mature for their age. As a result, both had enjoyed the sexual attention of nuns; so much so that, while Maria managed to remain a married woman, her daughter Serina found that the sexual life she shared with her husband was deficient and within a couple of years she found herself happily single again.

Now they enjoyed themselves in a variety of ways. Maria and Serina sometimes worked together as maids and kitchen hands for wealthy people, discovering that a few bored society ladies welcomed the opportunity to explore the bisexual aspect of themselves. A couple of these ladies regularly phoned and suggested it was time for one or both of them to pop over for coffee, cake and a little bit of fun. Sometimes they arranged to meet the two at a friend's beach house or some other location. One offered them her husband's cock, just for something a little different. When Maria and Serina did make visits, they took along sex toys in their bags and introduced their clients to a rich lesbian experience, although some of the woman they visited where able to teach Maria and her daughter a few things too.

They also enjoyed Grandpa Alberto, much to his appreciation.

Alberto was blessed with good health and a very large and healthy cock, which both women were happy to handle lovingly. Nono Alberto slept a lot and spent much time outside in his garden.

Now they had Sister Janice, their new nun, just like the ones at school. With thoughts about their experiences with their attentive teachers, both wanted to devour Sister Janice as they had been taught to enjoy their teachers.

"Argh!" sighed Maria. "Sister Janice, you are beautiful. Say you will stay with us for a few days. Grandpa will love you as we do, and you will love him, especially his lovely cock."

Serina removed her mouth from Janice's and Janice whispered her response.

"That sounds wonderful, Maria. I'd love to spend time here, just so long as you both don't mind teaching me as much you can about sex and love. I want to make up for lost time and you are both so beautiful. And your Nono sounds exciting too. I've never seen a man's cock."

5

JANICE ENJOY'S HER BREAKFAST

JANICE WAS QUITE comfortable telling a lie or two as she moved her hand back between Maria's soft thighs and felt the wetness on her fingers. But Janice reminded herself once again that she must play the part of the innocent virgin nun who knew nothing about sex.

This masquerade she had thought up at Mary's party was already looking to be more exciting than she had imagined and Janice revelled in the idea that her two new ladies thought it was like having access to their misbehaving boarding-school nuns, from their younger days.

The delightfully lecherous Janice was intent on having every erotic stimulus that was on offer, and she would endeavour to satisfy herself and her new lovers in every way she could.

Janice awoke to the smell of fresh coffee. She felt very relaxed, probably from the fervent attention she had received the night before from her new lady friends. She leisurely touched herself between her legs, remembering the enthusiasm with which they welcomed her into their home.

She left the bed and saw that her clothes had been washed and folded and her stockings and garter belt hung from the back of a chair beside which sat her shoes.

Janice showered then wandered around as she dried herself, looking around at the sparse furnishings. Sets of drawers stood at either side of the bed. In the top drawer of one she discovered a vast array of dildos, every one designed for a specific purpose. Some had flanges on the ends making them usable with a harness. One had a finger-like appendage, which pointed to and touched a clitoris when in use. Most were coloured in pink or blue or purple. Some were translucent with gold or silver flecks set in them.

In the back of a drawer, Janice spied what looked like a box for posting bottles of wine. On the outside in big letters was written the name 'Geraldine'.

Janice opened the box and discovered not one but two very long and thick black rubber dildos. She gently removed one from the box, handling it lovingly. Then Janice opened her mouth very wide and put the end of it between her lips, closed her eyes and made little sucking noises, smiling inside as she brought up fantasy images from past encounters. In the drawer below were dildo harnesses and these, too, where in bright colours, but mostly red or black.

Then she went to the other side of the bed. The first drawer was also full of sex toys. What took her eye in particular were the strapless dildos, with the large lump at one end which fitted inside a vagina. These could be held down under panties so that one could go anywhere knowing that one was prepared for sudden adventures and could spring into action the minute one pulled one's knickers aside or down.

Then there were butt plugs and small dildos designed for bottom play, along with some things she hadn't ever seen but sort of knew about. One was a smallish pink V-shaped soft thingy used for clitoral self-pleasuring and the other was a soft spongy thing with lips. The idea was that your clit went between the lips and you pumped the device with your fingers to make it suck you.

As Janice prepared to leave, she stopped to peep into a walk-in wardrobe. It was full of dresses and skirts and dress-up clothes including at least three maids' outfits and a sexy looking lady Santa outfit. Christmas party revelry, she thought. There was also a large range of shoes and boots. Then she noticed something else. Hanging behind the door were two fine leather switches and a wooden spanking paddle hung on a hook beside them.

Sister Janice was impressed. This boudoir was a pleasure centre *par excellence.*

Janice left the bedroom in search of coffee and something to eat.

"Good morning, Sister Janice! This is Father Munro. He's retired and totally deaf."

Janice had arrived in the kitchen to find Maria dressed in just a dressing gown and little Chinese slippers and standing at the stove making breakfast.

"There is muesli on the bench. Would you like bacon and eggs, or I can offer you toast with marmalade or strawberry jam? And how do you take your coffee?"

"A caffe latte would be good, Maria, and toast and marmalade please."

Janice looked at the elderly priest sitting at the breakfast bench. He was busy eating his bacon and eggs and didn't seem to notice Janice's arrival. He was a well-preserved older man, probably in his mid-seventies. Janice went and sat on a stool beside him.

Father Munro looked up and saw Janice smiling at him, he smiled back and continued eating. Maria came over with a coffee for the priest. Then she stood looking and smiling at Janice.

"Did you sleep well, Sister Janice? I hope you did. We did. I hope we didn't frighten you. Serina and I just couldn't get enough of you and we might have been a bit rough."

Janice looked back at Maria and fixed her with a gentle, loving smile, wishing she could blush on demand.

"Well, I did love it, Maria. And you were not too rough. I will look back on my first sexual encounter with the two of you as one of the luckiest and loveliest days of my life."

Maria came around the breakfast bar and put her arms out and

Janice welcomed her with a loving hug. Then Janice asked Maria to kiss her and Maria did so with enthusiasm, while Janice slipped her hand inside Maria's dressing gown and caressed her breasts and felt her shudder.

"Stop it, darling. I don't want to stop, but there are things I must do. We will have time together later. I promise."

Maria smiled at Janice and moved back into the kitchen.

"Father Munro comes to visit once a month. We give him a little bit of attention, so to speak."

Maria threw Janice a knowing look.

"We enjoy it and so does he. But since we moved in here as caretakers, he hasn't been able to get an erection on any of his two visits so far. This is his third visit. I've played with it and put his hand between my legs, wriggled my bare backside in front of his face, but nothing seems to work. I don't know what more we can do, really."

Maria picked up a pencil and writing pad from the kitchen bench and started to write, speaking as she went.

"Because he's so deaf, I write him messages. I'm just letting him know who you are."

Then she took the pad and laid it beside Father Munro's plate for him to read and went back to making toast and coffee for Janice.

Janice thought for a moment and chose her words carefully. "Oh, how sad. I wonder if it's to do with your new accommodation? Maybe it just doesn't feel the same as your old place?"

Maria called back as she moved some things in the fridge.

"You could be right, Janice."

"Maria? If Father Munro hasn't got an erection, and I have never seen a penis, perhaps it would be a good opportunity for me to see his now so that I at least know what a limp one looks like. What do you think, Maria? Would it be improper for me to do that?"

Maria laughed. "You are so sweet, Sister Janice. Of course you can have a look. Have a feel too while you're there. His trousers are down around his ankles already. I'm sure he wouldn't mind."

Janice rejoiced in Maria's easygoing attitude and looked at the man sitting beside her. He was reading Maria's note. When he had finished it, he turned and looked at Janice and beamed a very big smile.

"Nice to meet you, Sister Janice," he said, holding out his hand.

Janice shook Father Munro's hand and smiled and mouthed a suitable reply.

"Nice to meet you too, Father".

So! He believed she was a nun too. What fun. Janice was intrigued. What was going on in the elderly priest's head? She was soon to find out.

Janice dismounted from the kitchen stool and squatted down beside the priest's hairy legs, and stared into the shadows. There, nestled in between his thighs was a mass of curly hair and, almost hidden in the middle and only just visible, she could see his shrivelled penis. Janice pretended to gasp.

"Oh my God! Maria! I can see it. I'm not sure what to do next. Please advise me, Maria."

"All right Sister Janice. Don't panic. Help is at hand. I'll be there in a moment."

Maria came around the bench and looked at Janice crouched down with her tight skirt pulled up and staring at Father Munro's cock. She also stared at Janice's divine legs and feet, knowing that she and Serina would feast on Sister Janice again later.

She lifted Janice's hand and placed it on top of the priest's cock and whispered.

"There, darling. Now just run your thumb and fingers over the top of it. You can also reach in underneath and find his balls and rub those. He loves having his balls rubbed. Now I'm just about to serve your toast and coffee, so don't be too long."

After just a few moments feeling the priest's genitals, Janice surface and sat back on her stool.

"Well, Maria! That was interesting. Thank you."

Maria replied, laughing.

"We'll find you an erect one later, darling. I think you will find that far more interesting."

Not long after Janice had started eating her toast and sipping her coffee, she felt a hand sliding up her stockinged leg, a strong hand that seemed to know where it was going. She said nothing. Janice let things stay as they were for a minute or two, enjoying the experience and wondering what Father Munro had in mind. Then a finger slipped into her panties and caressed her pussy. Janice thought she should respond with some encouragement, if only to be polite.

As Janice lifted her arm and hand from the table top and moved it down towards her leg, the priest's other hand came across and took hers and carried it across and wrapped her fingers around a very serviceable boner. A sharp thrill of surprise and pleasure ran through her genitals and Janice reminded herself once again that she must, under all circumstances, maintain her innocent persona.

"Maria?"

"Yes, darling? More toast?"

"Er, not now. There are things happening under the bench that you might need to come and help me with, Maria. Father Munro has got an erection."

Maria turned and stared at Janice. "Is that a joke, Janice?"

"No, it's not. He has just put my hand on it and I need your help please, Maria."

Maria walked over and round and looked at what was happening. She bent down and looked at Janice's hand on Father Munro's cock.

"Well, that is very interesting, Sister Janice. You obviously have the touch."

"Or maybe Father has a special interest in nuns?" replied Janice. "Did you say I was a nun on your note?" Janice reached out and pulled the writing pad over and read the words "Sister Janice".

"Yes I did. I think you might be right. So what would you like to do with it, Sister Janice? It's your call. I imagine that if I tried to take over, he might not appreciate it and lose his erection."

"I wonder what he did with other nuns, if he had them?" wondered Janice, speaking quietly.

Maria laughed. "I think you need to take the lead Sister Janice. Father has the hots for a nun and you need to respond in a way that suits you."

"Advise me please, Maria. I need help now. This is all very new to me and I'm a little nervous."

"Well, your options are: rubbing his cock and masturbating him, known as a hand job; or you could suck him off, known as a blow job;

or let him put his cock into your cunt and you let him fuck you. Or you could write, 'no thanks' on the pad and make sure he reads it."

Janice looked at Maria with a pleading face.

"If you turned your back on him, Maria, and I lifted your dressing gown and you bent over and I guided his erection into your pussy, he would be a happy man, I'm sure. Can we try that, Maria? Please? I'm a bit lost."

Maria looked at the worried Janice.

"Yes, let's see what we can do. I do enjoy Father Munro's cock and haven't had him for ages. Yes, we'll try that."

Maria turned around and bent forward over a bar stool and Janice lifted Maria's dressing gown right up and rested it on her shoulders. She looked at Maria's shapely legs and backside and smiled with appreciation. Then she put her hand between Maria's legs and whispered, "You are so beautiful, Maria."

"Oh, Sister Janice. Please keep me in after class and do whatever you want to do with me," whispered Maria in a mock schoolgirl voice.

Janice could not stop herself. Moving momentarily into the role of Maria's teacher was very exciting given Maria's response.

"I will, young lady. You can be assured of that. Now keep your hands away from your pussy until I can get to you."

Maria shuddered as the role-playing words from Janice found their mark.

"My God, Janice. You make role play more wonderful than the real thing. Can't wait to get more."

"Be quiet, child. Now! Try Father Munro's cock in the meantime. I promised him my sluttiest pupils pussy. Keep still, and when he yells, call out "yes Father" and "More please Father", in a loud voice." Janice's stern instructions made Maria utter a tiny scream.

"Sister Janice, you are priceless. I'm coming already."

Janice slowly dragged Father Munro onto his feet and turned him to face Maria's rear end. Then, still holding his cock, she nuzzled the end of it against the lovely woman's moist pink slit which nestled serenely in the midst of her profuse black pubic hair. Her cunt opened and Janice slipped the priest's cock into Maria.

It worked. Within moments, Father Munro was pounding Maria's vulva with gusto, yelling as he did, "There, Sister, take all of it. And make sure you come to the confessional during the week and I'll fuck you again. I know you love it."

"Yes, Father. Yes, I will! I love it. Give it to me harder, Father," Maria called out over her shoulder and in a voice loud enough for the priest to hear

Janice stood in front of Maria and the two smiled lovingly at each other. Janice had her hand up her skirt, then she lifted it and pulled her panties to her knees to let Maria see her playing with herself amidst her modest blonde curls.

Maria put out her arms and let her hands and fingers enjoy the feel of Janice's slowly rocking, mesmerising long legs, and her thighs.

Janice and Maria and Father Munro all came at the same time. The priest fell back down on his seat and the two women embraced and kissed each other.

"That was so good, Sister Janice," said a rather breathless Maria, sliding a hand over her very wet cunt.

"I thought so too, Maria. My sexual experiences are getting better every minute, thanks to you."

Maria picked up the notebook and wrote the word "Football?" and pushed it over to the now sleepy-looking priest.

"Yes, please!" called Father Munro as Maria straightened her dressing gown and headed back to the kitchen bench to put on more coffee.

Maria came over and took the priest's hand and led him through the doorway leading to a passageway that led to the sitting room and the giant television.

When she came back she looked at Janice and laughed.

"All men enjoy the simple pleasures of life, darling. Sex and football. And not always in that order."

6

JANICE GETS A JOB

"Now I wonder where Serina is. I expected her back by now. Father Munro's social activities officer will be here to collect him some time soon, and Serina will miss her."

Maria looked closely at Janice with a questioning look on her face.

"What is it, Maria? Is something wrong?"

Maria smiled.

"No, darling! Nothing is wrong. I was thinking whether I could ask you to stand in for Serina if she doesn't turn up, but I think you're probably not quite ready for it yet."

Janice made sure that she was looking sufficiently innocent.

"If you are thinking about something sexual, Maria, I'm up for it. Watching you shagging Father Munro gave me great confidence that I should be able to do anything you put in front of me. I'm sorry that I responded to Father's erection the way I did, but now I've seen what happens, I'm pretty much ready for anything."

Maria smiled and eyed Janice quizzically.

"Well, Janice. I don't know whether you know what a dildo is. It's a rubber cock that we women sometimes strap around our waists to fuck each other with. It feels good, better than a real cock sometimes, although not always."

Again Maria studied Janice's face for a response.

"Good heavens, Maria. It sounds wonderful. Can you show me one?"

Maria smiled.

"Yes, Sister, I can and I will. I should mention that dildos come in various sizes and shapes. You use them with plenty of lubricant.

"Serina loves me to do her with one on most mornings before she leaves her bed. She can get quite sulky sometimes if I don't give it to her. She says she needs it to wake up and face the day."

Janice listened enthusiastically.

"Perhaps she would let me try giving it to her tomorrow morning, Maria? What a wonderful experience it would be for a novice. Would you mind if I asked her?"

"Be my guest, Sister Janice. But I might have to be there to help. You can have both of us. Just to help you with your practice of course."

Both women laughed out loud.

"Now Serina still isn't here and Father Munro's welfare officer could be here any minute. Serina is Geraldine's favourite. Not sure how I'll manage if she doesn't get home in time."

Janice was suddenly excited. Was this the Geraldine who's name she had read on the box containing the giant dildos?

Sister Janice felt a little rush of excitement and anticipation.

The doorbell rang moments after the two women finished their conversation and Maria opened the door.

"Geraldine, darling. Do come in. I have bad news. Serina hasn't got back from her cleaning job yet. I'm very sorry."

Janice stared at the biggest woman she had ever seen. Geraldine was very tall, much taller than Janice, even in her regulation flat black brogues, and she must have been at least twice Janice's weight. She had cropped spiky blonde hair with random streaks of blue and red and she had piercing bright blue eyes. A vine leaf tattoo ran down her neck and disappeared under the collar of a white shirt. She wore a uniform of sorts, like a suit, a blue jacket and skirt and a man's tie, yellow with little crucifixes.

"Geraldine! I'd like you to meet Sister Janice. Sister has recently left a convent to discover life, so to speak. She's not sure what to do next but luckily for her, and us, we found her so she is spending a little time here until she can find employment."

Geraldine stared back at Janice, showing no emotion or clue to her thoughts.

"Well, that is interesting. But first things first Maria. I can't stay. I have an important meeting at midday, so I'll grab Father Munro and head back to the retirement centre. Tell Serina that I'm sorry I missed her but look forward to seeing her next time."

Then Geraldine fixed her eyes on Janice.

"Do you have any skills other than the Church, Sister Janice? Can you type or use a computer?"

Janice was taken aback by Geraldine's forthrightness, but responded quickly, once again reminding herself of her new innocent persona.

"Well yes, Geraldine. I teach music, play piano and organ and yes, I can type and use a computer."

Janice smiled and the giant woman managed to smile back.

"Fine! If you would like to see me in my office on Wednesday at 3 pm, I will interview you. I'm looking for a personal assistant, but our limited budget demands that I find a multi-skilled person also capable of helping with the residents and the staff. We have around thirty priests. Are you interested?"

Maria looked back and forth at both of them.

"The retirement centre is very close to here Sister. You could board with us until you knew what you wanted to do about accommodation."

Janice thought very quickly, swiftly reorganising her other life as she did so. She had music teaching commitments, but mostly her work times were flexible. And this offer looked as if it might well afford her more sensual excitement. Janice's lustful needs always came first.

"Thank you, Geraldine. Yes, I would like to come and see you. Thank you."

Geraldine looked at Maria and asked her to give Janice her phone number so that she could text if need be.

"Send me your contact details, Sister."

Maria reached up and kissed Geraldine.

"That is so kind of you, darling. Now let's go get the priest."

Janice arrived at the Catholic Retirement Centre for retired clergy for her job interview just before three o'clock as arranged. She felt a little unsure of herself.

Going for a job was all new to her. It was many years since she had worked in a regular job, and that had only ended when Janice was discovered in the store room, her naked breasts rubbing against another woman's naked breasts and their hands up each other's skirts. The fact that the other woman was the boss's wife made things very much worse than they might have been.

Janice smiled to herself, remembering a long-past lustful moment, triggered only because she was here for a job interview.

She found the door marked Chief Officer and knocked. Geraldine opened the door and she went in.

When Janice had met Geraldine at Maria's house, she had thought how scary the woman seemed. She imagined her as the classic dominatrix. Not that Janice didn't have time for such things. Being a subservient plaything for a mistress appealed to Janice's most base instincts, as did the idea of playing the role of a dominant mistress. She had enjoyed many memorable moments disciplining someone. Even the husband of the aforementioned breast rubbing wife, she recalled.

7

THE WORK ROUTINE

"TAKE A SEAT, Janice, and may I just say how nice you look. Now tell me, did Maria and Serina teach you about dildo's after we met?"

Janice thought quickly, then moved straight into the Sister masquerade mode, innocent but keen to know more about the real world and, in particular, sensuality.

"Oh yes, Geraldine. And I most certainly enjoyed it. I think I got the hang of it but I do need more practice."

The striking figure behind the desk smiled approvingly.

"Well Sister Janice. You will be getting plenty of practice here as part of your job."

Janice's pussy trembled a little, reminding her of the pleasure she'd had on the two previous nights, when Maria and Serina had led her to the bedroom after dinner.

"Follow us Sister Janice," they whispered, laughing excitedly as they anticipated introducing the beautiful Sister Janice to her first dildo experience.

Geraldine rose and reached over and took Janice's hand and led her through a doorway at the back of the office. It led to a pleasantly furnished room. With Chintz curtains, a big bed, a white fluffy carpet and an ensuite bathroom, it provided an ideal hideaway.

Geraldine turned to Janice.

"I want you to take off your panties, Sister Janice so that I can properly interview you for the position I have planned for you."

Janice waited only a moment before she lifted her skirt and, with both hands, slid down her knickers and stood with a growing feeling of excitement.

Then she watched excitedly as Geraldine disrobed, hanging her clothes on hangers and putting them in the wardrobe.

What an amazing sight! Geraldine removed her shoes and stood up, tall and vivacious. She wore a bright red brassiere and panties set. Her extraordinarily shapely body seemed to fill the room and Janice could smell her warmth and perfume.

"Do you like what you see, Sister? This body needs servicing every morning at around nine thirty, and I'm hoping you will be the one to do it. Come here and let me feel you."

Janice moved towards Geraldine. The woman put her hands down and ran them up under Janice's skirt.

"Take everything off, Janice. Let me see what I'm going to get each morning."

Janice stripped off and pirouetted in front of her new boss. Geraldine stared at Janice's extraordinary bubble butt and her impossibly long slim legs.

"Beautiful! Now come on the bed and lie on top of me Janice. But first remove my bra and undies, then lay your cunt on my face so that I can smell you."

Janice did as she was told. She had expected that Geraldine would be rough with her, but Geraldine seemed entirely reasonable, not at all the violent, demanding monster that she had imagined.

She took off Geraldine's bra and then her panties. Then she stared at Geraldine's incredibly beautiful body. The vine leaf visible on her neck was part of a complete grapevine tattoo that ran down her back, around her belly, then branched into two and meandered down her thighs, ending at her ankles.

Geraldine was a woman who obviously worked out, but without exhibiting the massive muscling that some women of her persuasion liked to develop. Her skin was taut all over, and her breasts were so perfect that Janice assumed that Geraldine had had a boob job. But false or not, they were too impressive to ignore. They were huge and stood out and up, and her dark brown nipples were long and stiff and begged for attention.

Janice wanted to play with Geraldine's tits for the rest of the day. They were truly monumental. Her nipples stood up and screamed for a willing mouth. Geraldine backed onto the bed and lay down.

"Come along, Sister. I'm waiting for you."

Janice climbed on top of Geraldine, turned her backside and lowered her pussy onto the woman's face. A muffled groan issued from the head between Janice's legs, and the gigantic body lying beneath her, moved like a horse rolling on the grass, as horses so often do after being unsaddled and let loose.

Janice had her arms wrapped around Geraldine's abdomen with her hands clasping two gigantic taut buttocks. She searched around, inspecting every part of Geraldine's legs and her beautiful belly. Then she put her head down, daring to put it between Geraldine's thighs in search of her secret places.

"Yes, you beautiful bitch. Lick my cunt."

Janice was already there, pushing through a swath of blond hair, sniffing and wiggling her nose and chin in the moist undergrowth.

"Yes, Oh yes! Please! Do whatever. Just do it!"

Geraldine was now lapping Janice's wet pussy and nibbling on her clit and Janice was in heaven. This was what she lived for; sensation and the anticipation of another climax. Her fingers were now working their magic inside Geraldine's vulva and the woman's lower body trembled and moved dramatically, its huge size giving force to every movement.

Geraldine began sobbing loudly, as if it was something she always did, and Janice felt her sexual power surge.

Knowing that Geraldine was finding satisfaction made Janice decide to move forward. She placed four fingers into Geraldine's giant soaking wet vulva and moved her entire hand inside her. And she didn't rest there. Slowly she moved her hand in further until her forearm was half inside Geraldine's body. Then, after resting for a moment, she ever so slowly turned her now clenched fist, first a little to the left and then a little to the right.

Geraldine exploded; then, moments later, she exploded again and then again. She kept on climaxing until Janice thought she might do herself an injury. In the meantime, Janice was climaxing regularly from having Geraldine's mouth glued to her cunt.

A moment came when both women were lying still, just resting.

"Geraldine, I'm going to take my hand out. I'm not sure whether it should be in there for that long."

There was a moments silence. Then a croaky voice spoke.

"Leave it where it is, darling. I haven't finished yet."

Janice smiled.

"Just as long as your comfortable Geraldine. I love having it there. And Geraldine? Being with you is like being in heaven. I love it. Oh, and Geraldine? I want you to lay on top of me. I would love that."

"Tomorrow, darling. I have a meeting shortly."

It didn't take Janice long to find her way around the retirement centre. After Geraldine had confirmed her position and appointed Janice as her personal assistant, music and games activities administrator, staff welfare officer and, of course, her personal sex slave, Janice surveyed her new domain and she liked what she saw.

She had been given accommodation and a work area away from the residents' units, but only a short distance from the staff room. It was really a large and comfortable lounge room with two sofas and three arm chairs, and it included a piano. A bedroom was attached, containing a double bed, wardrobes and an ensuite.

Part of her round of duties was to make short visits to priests to check on their welfare. The retirement centre housed some thirty retired priests in two different wings of the building. One wing was for those requiring some form of regular care, while the other housed the healthy priests who required only feeding and a little home help.

This second group spent a lot of time socialising away from the retirement centre.

Janice began each morning with her boss, Geraldine. It took only a few days of practice before Geraldine declared that Sister Janice was a 'dildo natural'.

Her first day at work saw the two women naked in Geraldine's special room. At first they stood with their lips glued to each other's and their hands palming each other's pussies. Then Geraldine opened a drawer and brought out a giant dildo, like those Janice had seen in the drawer at Maria's house.

Geraldine stood in front of Janice, then bent down and lifted each of Janice's legs to slip on the harness, tightening the buckles as she went. It was just a moment of subservience to her boss, but while Geraldine fiddled with the harness she allowed Janice the opportunity to fondle her beautiful breasts, and hurriedly sucking on a hard nipple before being dragged to the bed by her giant lesbian lover.

"Now Sister Janice, imagine me lying naked in front of the altar and you are the lecherous nun who came in for a quick Hail Mary and seeking forgiveness after you had just sexually enjoyed two of your fellow novices. Your pussy is still wet and you are craving more juicy playthings. You can have me now, Sister Janice. I'm ready for you."

Janice needed no further encouragement. She hoisted herself up between Geraldine's large thighs and nestled the end of the huge dildo in her mass of pubic hair.

"Put your legs in the air, you beautiful wet bitch," Janice whispered, before her mouth engulfed a stiff nipple.

Geraldine lifted her legs high into the air.

"Whatever you want, Sister Janice. Do what ever you want girl, just so long as you push that fucking thing into me, right now."

Janice pushed and the giant cock slid all the way in. Then she lifted herself upwards and drove the dildo down hard, sending it much further in.

Geraldine screamed.

"Oooh! My God, that feels so good, Janice. Don't ever stop doing this to me you skinny, leggy bitch."

Janice lifted herself up again and pushed down hard. Geraldine screamed.

While Janice worked her dildo in and out of her sex-hungry boss, she licked, tugged and sucked Geraldine's beautiful breasts. Geraldine orgasmed for the umpteenth time.

"Janice, I don't want us to stop, but I must get on with running the retirement centre. I said I'd lie on top of you the other day. Would you like me to do that now, to finish off? I'm happy to do it."

Janice heard what Geraldine had said and slowly extricated the dildo from her boss's cunt.

"I would love it, Geraldine. I've been dreaming of it."

Janice rolled off Geraldine and lay back with her legs apart. Geraldine was on top of her in moments, one hand offering a huge breast back to Janice's mouth, the other arm around Janice's buttocks, pulling them together as she rubbed herself against her new personal assistant's pubic mound.

"There, you sexy PA. Tomorrow I'll shag you just like you shagged me. Gotta go to work now, sweetie."

"Don't go! I'm coming!"

Janice screamed and pushed upwards and Geraldine joined her, crushing her as she thrust wildly against her. Then both women sighed and slid about on their sweaty bodies, not wanting things to end.

"That was a lovely finale darling," Geraldine giggled. "I didn't know I could do that."

8

NURSING AIDES

HALF A DOZEN or more nursing aides had fallen in love with Sister Janice in the first week. The moment these diminutive girls laid eyes on her long legs, she became the main topic of conversation.

Janice had been told how all of this group of young women had been together in the same convent school in Manila. Girls rushed to say hello in the mornings, and one girl had a picture taken of herself kneeling beside Janice's legs, her arms clasped around them and smiling cheerily.

As soon as this image appeared on the phones of her friends, every nurse wanted a similar selfie. Janice couldn't walk down the corridor without two girls rushing up to her, pleading to be allowed to kneel down and embrace her legs.

Selfies were the main focus on the young women's media posts and suddenly Sister Janice, or rather her long stockinged legs and high heels, were as popular among the girls as the latest fashion or pop star images. Janice couldn't help but enjoy the adoration.

If she had wondered about how she might enjoy these attractive young things more intimately, she didn't have to wait long for an answer.

Janice was staying in her own flat in Surrey Hills on Friday and Saturday nights, at Maria's and Serina's place on Sunday and Monday nights, and at her retirement centre apartment on the other days of the week. Everything about her life seemed to have fallen into place very quickly after she had met Maria and Serina at Mary's birthday party.

It was a Wednesday evening, and Janice was watching television in her apartment when she heard giggling outside in the passage followed moments later with a tentative knock on the door.

"Come in."

The door slowly opened just a little and two smiling faces peered around it and across the room at her.

"We brought you a plant, Sister Janice. And we thought you might be lonely too. We hope you don't mind us calling in?"

Two of her admirers came into the room, one carrying a plant pot containing an ornamental chilli plant, covered in a profusion of small red chillies.

"How nice of you both, I love having visitors, and goodness me, What a wonderful plant."

Janice waved the two to the settee across from her and switched off the television.

"Now let me see? It's Angel and Nicole, isn't it? I'm still trying to memorise all of your names."

Janice stared at the two across the room. A low diffused light came from the table lamp next to the TV, and she smiled as she looked at the young women looking at her and smiling, one behind her large polka dot-rimmed glasses, the other sporting a monumental set of white teeth.

"Yes, Sister Janice. You got our names right. It must be quite difficult remembering everybody's names to start with."

Nicole was going to be the talkative one, Janice thought.

"We seem to be so far away from you over here, Sister. May we come over there and sit beside you? Please?"

"Of course you can. I was thinking the same thing. Come over here."

Janice moved to the middle of the sofa and patted a hand on either side. The two young aides moved over and sat close, both with their beaming faces turned towards her.

"Do you ever get lonely, Sister Janice?"

Janice thought about what might be going on in the minds of her visitors and decided to engage them emotionally, earlier rather than later.

"As a matter of fact Nicole, I get very lonely at times. Especially at the end of a working day, when all you lovely ladies leave off work and I'm suddenly alone here in my room. I suppose I'm a bit spoilt. I do get a lot of loving attention during working hours so I really have no right to complain."

Janice looked at the face of each girl. Nicole with the big glasses and Angel with the big smile and a mouthful of shiny white teeth. Both had changed out of their uniforms and were now in identical pleated skirts and white blouses and long white socks.

If the members of this group of young women had been together in school in Manila, then it helped to explain their camaraderie and their familiarity with each other. It might also explain the identical clothes they were wearing.

It didn't really explain the make-up, though. Both girls had over-done the bright red lipstick and Janice could smell the face powder and heavy perfume. She guessed that they were still learning about life in the outside world, away from convent restraints and dress codes.

Nicole took Janice's hand and moved her face closer.

"We don't want you to ever feel lonely, Sister Janice, do we Angel?"

"No we don't, Sister. We could visit you regularly or whenever you want us to. We would love to spend time with you, Sister Janice."

Angel's hand closed on Janice's other hand and Janice sat admiring the two.

"Well, you two girls are just wonderful. I do so appreciate your concern. Maybe you both could call on me on a Wednesday night. I would look forward to that."

"Oh yes, Sister. We would love to have a regular date with you, wouldn't we, Angel?"

The girl with the big teeth smiled even wider.

"Oh, yes. We would love that."

"Now! Is there something you would like to do? Feel free to just relax and do whatever you want. And anything you want, just ask. And you are welcome to explore the fridge. There could be something there that you fancy."

Janice laughed and said, "And I'm quite happy if you just want to play with your smartphones. We can pretend we are a family and just do our thing or whatever."

Janice thought for just a moment before announcing, "Oh yes! To celebrate our first date, would either of you mind if I hugged and kissed you? I just want to feel close to you and taste your lipsticks."

They all laughed enthusiastically and the two girls moved their bodies as one, sitting up straight in anticipation.

"Please hug and kiss us, Sister Janice. But please don't be put off if we giggle. It just means we're excited," said Nicole.

"Or nervous," added Angel.

There was a pause, then Janice turned to Nicole and removed her glasses, leaning across her and placing them on the side cupboard. She put one arm around Nicole's shoulders and drew her close and then, with her other hand, lifted Nicole's face up so that she could look into her eyes.

"You are very beautiful, Nicole."

Then Janice moved her head forward and placed her lips firmly on the young woman's lips. Then she slowly ran her tongue along Nicole's bottom lip and did the same to the now trembling girl's top lip.

She felt Angel's hand looking for a spot to rest on the top of her leg.

She kept her mouth on Nicole's and was rewarded. Nicole pushed her tongue into Janice's and their tongues danced lovingly in their mouths.

"Is it my turn yet?" Angel's little voice whispered excitedly from behind Janice's head.

Janice slowly unfolded herself from the delightful and, by the sound of her deep breathing, excited Nicole and turned towards Angel.

Bright red big lips framed a huge set of beautiful white teeth. So large were the girl's molars, it seemed that she would never properly be able to close her mouth. This in no way made her less attractive; in fact, she just always looked as though she wanted to eat you, and the feeling from Janice was mutual.

Sister Janice put her arms around the larger girl then lifted Angel's head and placed her already wet lips firmly over the girl's mouth and in no time, she and Angel were loving each other's tongues. The only sound was that of Angel's stifled sighs along with Nicole's heavy breathing.

The lustful Janice had worked out where she wanted them all to go next. How to get there was now the challenge.

The three women lay back on the sofa. None of them wanted to stop their lovemaking, but none wished to make a move for fear of doing something the others might not be comfortable with.

Each had loved their kissing. But what should they do next? There was an awkward silence.

"Sister Janice? We loved being kissed by you. It was amazing," Nicole said quietly, looking across at her friend Angel.

"Sister Janice?"

"Yes, Angel?"

"Is there anything you would like us to do, Sister? Anything at all? We love being with you, so can we do something loving to you, Sister Janice?"

Janice looked at the two gorgeous and more than willing young ladies on either side of her, and savoured the moment. She took a little time to reply.

"Kissing you both has left me feeling something I haven't felt for years, a yearning for a closer physical bonding with women. Can I ask you both to do something to help me with these feelings? And please don't judge me harshly. I'm feeling a little vulnerable at this moment."

There was silence and then Nicole answered.

"Anything! Ask us for anything, Sister Janice. We would love to make you happy in any way you want. Anything at all!"

Janice looked into the dark eyes of the girl with the big teeth and smile, then she turned and looked into the doe-eyed short-sighted beauty on her left.

"I'm not sure how to say this, but here goes. I would love it if you helped me take off my undies and then let me watch each of you take off yours.

"I've always believed that at the end of the day, we women can relax much better that way. But if you would prefer not to do that, I'm fine with that too. I just love being here with you both. And I also want to kiss you both some more."

There was a pause while the two girls looked at each other and smiled, and then, as one, they slid to the floor and reached their hands up beneath Sister Janice's skirt, with each planting a kiss on Janice's knees as they did so.

In just moments they had her knickers down. Angel took Janice by the ankles and lifted her legs and Nicole slid the panties down over her ankles and shoes and tossed them onto an armchair.

The two girls stood up and stared down at Sister Janice as she nestled down into the sofa cushions. Then Janice smiled up at them reached down and lifted her skirt up over her belly, displaying her little auburn patch. She watched the two girls staring at her wide-eyed, their mouths gaping. Then she put one hand down between her legs and closed her eyes.

"Thank you, Angel and Nicole. That feels so much better, but now I want to see you both without your knickers and feel your lips on mine. Hurry, my darlings, I want more kissing."

The two girls looked at each other, then instantly lifted their skirts and took down their panties and threw them away.

"Come and put your bare bottoms on my thighs, girls. I so want to feel your skin on mine."

Both the young women moved in unison, lifting their skirts as they parked their bottoms on their goddess's thighs.

Then they all embraced enthusiastically. The two girls leant towards each other, their mouths swallowing each others' tongues while Sister Janice ran her fingers up each girl's legs until she had a hand on both of their tiny bushes, discovering that they were both exceedingly wet. Both girls moaned excitedly as Sister Janice fingered them.

"You have made me very happy and I love you both. Can I ask you if you will visit me again on a Wednesday evening, as we discussed? Tell me you will want more of this."

Both Angel and Nicole were now writhing on Sister Janice's fingers while they sucked each other's mouths. One began to undo the buttons of the other's blouse and the favour was returned. Both girls were soon able to rid themselves of another piece of clothing. Then they turned and took turns with Sister Janice's lips and mouth, unbuttoning her blouse as they went.

There was a moment when the girls separated and Nicole spoke.

"Sister Janice! We will definitely be here next Wednesday."

Then, as Nicole reached in to discover Sister Janice's breast and then her nipples, Angel added, "I think we might still be here. Oh God! I've never felt like this before in my whole life. You are both so beautiful."

Janice couldn't help but feel suddenly even more lustful, looking at the four tiny but shapely breasts calling to her. Her hands moved up and fondled them lovingly. The girls laughed and squealed and brazenly wriggled and pushed their breasts out to meet the mouth of their goddess.

Then Janice spread her legs wide apart and asked the girls to slide their pussies up and down on her long, stockinged legs.

Janice's legs were a source of excitement for her and for anyone who looked at them and the two girls immediately turned over and parted their legs, each straddling one of Sister Janice's long legs, first on a bare thigh and then moving slowly downwards over Janice's suspenders and silky stocking tops until they reached a knee. Janice's bony knees provided a sympathetic protrusion and greater traction for the two excited girls, and they eagerly rubbed themselves on them.

Nicole came first, along with a tiny scream, then Angel called out, "Me now! Oh God! Yes, Sister Janice!"

The two girls slumped forward onto Janice's tummy, clasping each other and kissing feverishly.

Janice was in heaven. After a minute or two, she whispered, "Would someone please lick me?"

Moments later, two mouths jostled for position, and two tongues slurped Janice's very wet pussy. Janice put her hands on the girls' heads, gently pulling them closer. Then she made a deep and lasting moaning sound and exploded.

When all had orgasmed and the girls had climbed up to lay their heads on Sister Janice's welcoming bosoms, and she was contentedly stroking their cheeks and licking each one's red lips in turn, she thought how beautiful their discovering each other had been.

Janice couldn't be sure if this was the first time that the girls had so intimately touched each other, but she felt sure it wouldn't be the last, with or without her participation.

Janice languidly put a hand on Angel's bare breasts and played with a tiny erect nipple. Angel opened her eyes and smiled, her big red lips and her enormous teeth beckoning Janice's mouth to come to hers.

As Janice attached herself to the girl, losing herself in a heavenly dance of tongues, Nicole's voice whispered in her ear.

"We are in love with you, Sister Janice. Now Angel? I think it's my turn? Please?"

"We are in love with you Sister Janice."

When Janice heard those words – and appreciated where they were coming from – she didn't realise that she was about to be launched into superstardom, at least with the nurses at the retirement centre.

Janice never found out whether it was Nicole or Angel who shared information about their visit to her apartment. It didn't really matter which one. Whoever it was must have mentioned their wonderful night out to one of the other nursing staff, probably "in strict confidence, of course", describing how she and another nurse had enjoyed a wonderful evening with the long-legged goddess, Sister Janice.

And so it came to pass that on the following Tuesday night, giggles were heard outside in the passageway followed by a knock on Sister Janice's door, and Sister Janice found herself with two more sweet young things in pleated skirts and white blouses and very lipsticked lips, inquiring about her welfare and. in particular, whether or not she was lonely.

Janice was taken aback by this so obvious attempt at seduction, especially when it was apparent from the start that she wouldn't really be required to seduce anybody, but simply issue instructions. These girls were bent on seducing themselves, like groupies throwing themselves at pop stars.

"Oh, how sweet of you both! Do come in and find a seat."

Janice looked the girls over. One was plumpish and giggled nervously while the other was slightly taller and more finely built and quietly confident. They held hands, which was not uncommon among these girls. Friendships were mostly very close and much valued in their culture.

As soon as Janice got over the initial shock of the girls' arrival, she set about thinking through what she would do and then, more importantly, what she would like to do to them and what she would like them to do to her.

"Now remind me who you two are. I see you often enough during work time, but as I'm new here I haven't yet mastered remembering everyone's names."

"I'm Louise," said the chubbier one in a nervous voice.

"And I'm Tina."

Janice was thinking fast. Given that these two knew why they were here, there was no need for her to carry on with the charade that depicted her as the sad and lonely woman. That was now irrelevant. Janice was suddenly having to think of a new approach. One that made sense but, most importantly, one that would give her whatever she felt she would like.

"Well, it's so kind of you both to call in. But the truth is, girls, I've had a rotten day and I don't think even you beauties can cheer me up."

9

IN LOVE WITH JANICE

JANICE WAS BEING HONEST. It had been a difficult day, beginning with the fire alarm going off at around nine forty-five, just as her boss was about to bring Janice to an orgasm.

"Fire alarm interruptus, darling. Sorry, Janice, I'll make it up to you later."

Then one of the bedridden priests died, and when the medics from the local hospital came to take him away, they discovered he was wearing a condom. Before anyone could do anything, the priest's niece had been informed and all hell broke loose with possible demands for an inquiry and a hint of legal action.

Janice made enquiries, then gave one of the Russian nurses time off and told her to just disappear. Then she was given the task of meeting the priest's niece.

Fortunately, Janice soon perceived the masculine looking country woman staring at her long legs. Acting on a hunch, it wasn't long before Janice had bent over in front of the woman and then turned and smiled her special smile, successfully seducing the more than willing niece.

The neatly dressed strong and shapely woman responded with great enthusiasm. In just moments, she had a hand firmly up Sister

Janice's skirt between her legs and the other hand pulling Janice's hair.

"You sexy bitch; lick my pussy first and then we'll talk."

Twenty minutes on, first with Janice bent over the desk, then on the sofa and on the floor, the niece agreed not take the matter of the condom any further, just so long as Janice came to her house once a month for afternoon tea and a romp.

The niece wrote her address on a card and handed it to Janice.

"And you might have to fuck my husband if he's home. I love watching him with other women."

As Janice told her boss later in the day, "A tough day, but it was all in the line of duty, Geraldine."

———

Now she had two gorgeous young dusky-skinned nurses staring at her and wanting to be entertained and she wasn't sure that she was up for it.

"If it made you feel better, Sister Janice, you could spank our bottoms. Sister Moran at school used to do it to us when she got upset, didn't she, Tina? And she always said she felt much better afterwards."

Janice looked at the cute chubby nurse with her big breasts pushing to get out of her blouse and her big red Cupid's bow lips, and thought that things might work out after all.

"We always hoped that one day she would show us her bottom and let us spank her, but it never happened did it, Louise? So, after she'd finished with us and left, we touched each others bottom's and played around with each other instead."

The two girls giggled, recalling times past.

Janice could see that they were both quite experienced and up for whatever she felt she wanted and, in this instance, it wasn't her hands on their bottoms. Well, not this week anyway.

She knew exactly what she wanted. She realised that, since the visit by Nicole and Angel, she had discovered a new fetish. Now, with these two beauties, she could have more of it.

When last week's girls had slid down Janice's legs and each one had orgasmed on a knee, she had felt the wetness soaking her stockings. And when she stripped for bed later that night, and routinely sniffed her stockings before popping them into a basin of water to wash and hang in the bathroom to dry, she discovered a wonderful odour on them that could only have come from the girls sliding their wet pussies down her leg and creaming on them.

Instead of washing them, Janice took her stockings to bed and popped them under her pillow and lay luxuriating in the scent of the girls while palming her pussy, and when she woke in the morning the girls' scent was still there. Janice loved it.

She patted the sofa on either side of her and the two new lipsticked ladies came and sat with her. Following the same routine as last week, she asked the girls to kiss her, then to take off her panties, and then to take off their own panties.

Then Janice got them to undo her top and free her breasts and then undo and throw away their own tops. Finally she instructed them to put their bare bottoms on her bare thighs and, just moments later, while they were all in a flurry of mutual kissing, Janice took each of the already damp, almost hairless pussies in her hands and fingered them gently. Janice saw how suddenly both girls were transfixed and had closed their eyes. She looked down at each ones fully exposed puffy and shiny wet and almost hairless vaginas, reminding herself that she would want to feast on them, but maybe on their next visit.

"Oh Sister, that is beautiful!" cried Tina. "Please don't stop."

Louise pushed even harder on Sister Janice's mouth while pinching her hard nipples, all the time twisting and turning her groin on her groping hand. Janice was ready and opened her legs wider.

"Now my, darlings. Sister would like you to turn yourselves over and slide slowly up and down on her legs. Please do that and don't stop until Sister tells you to."

Just as Janice had planned it, the two excited girls straddled a leg each and began rubbing, moaning gently as they hovered in a state of near orgasm. And each did orgasm. They came at the top of her stockings, well before her knees.

Janice watched their faces. Each one became contorted moments before release, then their mouths sagged open and Janice pulled a head down to her mouth. Slowly she felt the two girls' wetness, soaking the tops of her legs. Then she whispered in a croaky voice, as she too felt herself edging closer to coming:

"Don't you dare stop now, girls. Slide down a bit further. You are going to give me a lot more of your delicious juices yet."

The girls were now moving their crotches down to her knees. She moved her hands from holding their necks to holding their bottoms. She gently ran fingers up and down each one's crack, then slowly inserted a digit into each girl's soft and sweaty little anus. Both girls gasped and rubbed themselves even harder on Janice's legs. Both came within a few moments, letting down more moisture for Janice to sniff in bed. But she still wasn't finished.

"Rub your pussies on Sister's bony knees now, please. I do love that."

Janice felt them sliding down her leg; then when each girl arrived at a knee they both paused, discovering that something special was pushing into their pussies and was even rubbing against their clitorises.

Wriggling and pushing was now the order of the day on Janice's knees with these two sexually over stimulated girls moaning and sobbing and no longer able to control themselves.

Her fingers pushed further into Louise and Tina's bottoms, causing them to jump up and down, pounding themselves on her magic knees. Suddenly she felt them both flooding on her legs as they screamed and slumped onto her bosom, each lipsticked mouth seeking out and nibbling one of her nipples.

Janice lay back and quietly ordered them onto their knees on the floor to lick her.

It was only a few minutes before Janice threw herself upwards and came as both girls attempted to keep their mouths glued to her special place.

She lay back again, feeling her saturated stockings and smiling and thinking of the night ahead, seeing her nose already nestled into the odour of today's delights. Then she heard a voice from between her legs.

"We are in love with you, Sister Janice."

"Well, girls, you are welcome to come again, but it has to be only on Tuesdays."

"We'll be here for sure next Tuesday, Sister, won't we, Louise?"

"For sure!"

FROM RUSSIA WITH LOVE

THERE WERE a number of Russian and Middle European nurses working in the high care section of the unit. One of them, Anna, was the carer that Janice had sent away following the condom incident, when medics had discovered a condom on the body of a heart-attack patient.

Once she had solved the problem with the priest's niece, Janice contacted Anna and told her that she could come back to work. When she returned, Janice interviewed her to try to ensure that this didn't happen again.

"Take a set Anna. Now why on earth was the priest wearing a condom?" Janice asked.

The skinny woman with the beautiful face and amazing cheek-bones smiled.

"He said it would protect him from God's wrath."

Janice could see that the girl found the whole affair amusing, as she herself did on reflection.

"How did you come to be fucking him? From what I hear, he was unconscious most of the day and night anyway."

The girl eyed Janice, looking at her face and her legs and high heels, and came to the conclusion that Janice was probably like her, and so could be trusted.

"You might know what its like when you can't get a cock when you need one, Sister. If you see something that could do the job, you usually take it. I'm addicted to it, Sister. That is how God has made me."

Janice felt a quiver in her crotch and looked at Anna, letting her see that her sensuality was acknowledged and appreciated. Anna looked back and smiled.

"Is your appetite for cock a result of experiences you had in your younger days, Anna?"

"Probably. I lived with two older brothers and an alcoholic father and uncle. And then there were the neighbours. I was on call for pretty much twenty-four hours a day."

Janice thought about what life must have been like for Anna but couldn't imagine it. She tried to contrast it with what she knew about the convent girls she worked with. It seemed so different. Janice knew that the convent girls had early experiences with nuns and with each other, but surely it wouldn't have been so stark and unloving as the early experiences of this young woman.

"Didn't you try to get away somehow, Anna? Surely you could get help somewhere?"

Anna looked across the room and out of the window.

"I did. But not until I was sixteen. I applied for a job but then found myself being shipped off to London and locked up in a house as a sex worker.

"In some ways, playing with a man's cock at least once each day confirms my life and lets me feel complete. It's what I'm used to. Weird I know, but that's how it is."

Janice was fascinated by the young woman's story.

"You've been here in Australia for a while now Anna. Surely this new life has brought changes for you?"

Anna thought for a moment, crossing her long legs and pointing a heeled foot at Janice.

"Yes, Sister, I have discovered new feelings. I have discovered love.

Well, sort of. I share my emotional life with two special women. I do love women."

"But you said you were addicted to cocks? How does that work?"

Anna laughed.

"It sounds funny, doesn't it? It's as though I have an inbuilt need to be useful somewhere. Sucking a cock or fucking one is the only useful skill I ever learnt, apart from cooking."

"So you don't do it for pleasure, Anna?"

"Satisfying my need to be useful is sort of a pleasurable experience but not like having what I now call proper emotional sex. Proper sex is what I have with women and that is where I can express and share my loving feelings."

Janice found Anna fascinating.

"So do you live with your special women friends Anna?"

Anna looked at Janice thoughtfully.

"Yes I do, Sister. You probably know them – Veronika and Dina – they both work here. We have similar backgrounds and of course we share a common language."

Janice knew the two girls. Both beautiful Russian women, similarly long-legged and skinny.

"And do they know about your need for cock?"

Anna laughed as she tended to do each time Janice asked her questions about cocks.

"We had similar experiences in our early days. Russia is a land of vodka and hopeless men. Abuse is hard to avoid for young females. While Dina had a slightly less abusive early life, Veronika suffered as I did. She, too, left home and ended up as a sex worker but in Berlin. Both of them understand that much of their power is usually via their manipulation of men and mens cocks."

Janice started to thank Anna for coming in, deliberately smiling innocently at the beautiful girl as she thought befitted her managerial role.

"Thanks for coming in, Anna. And thanks for sharing part of your life story with me. I can only suggest that you be a little more careful with condoms in your future cock events." Anna laughed.

As Janice began to stand, Anna stood up in front of her. Then

Anna leant forward and kissed her. Janice hesitated, then pushed gently back on Anna's mouth. Anna moved a hand up and spread her fingers and lightly brushed her hand across Janice's chest.

"Perhaps we could catch up again soon, Sister Janice. I have much more that I would like to share with you."

The two sensual women looked longingly into each other's eyes.

Janice surrendered herself, she hoped, with dignity.

"I will schedule another and longer appointment so that we can better enjoy meeting up, Anna."

JANICE GETS HER MEN

IN THE BRIGHT MOONLIGHT, a late arrival at the party moved quietly around the garden. Many of the guests had either left or were having loving moments in their respective quarters.

The figure of the latecomer tottered on high heels and wavered from side to side. She stopped every few moments to listen, like a hunter in the forest at night. Then she heard a sound and turned towards it, walking more surely, knowing what she was looking for. She stopped to listen and there it was again.

"In vino veritas."

Then silence. Janice saw a cigarette burning not far away in the direction from which the sound had come and she headed towards it.

The summer house doors were wide open. Alberto was lying on the floor, bathed in moonlight and holding a bottle in his hand. He was happy. Nearby, his nephew Giorgio, recently arrived from Naples, sat smoking, thinking of who knows what.

Janice slid into view and stood between the two of them with her long thin silky stockinged legs and shiny black high heels catching the moonlight.

Janice stared first at old Alberto on the floor, then turned her head and stared at the younger man, still sitting and smoking a cigarette.

Speechless, both men stared back.

Without saying a word, Janice slowly pointed towards her crotch. She began to slowly unzip her dress, letting it fall to her feet. Next she pulled down her black silk panties over her suspenders and stepped out of them.

She lay down first beside Alberto, then Janice lifted herself up onto her elbows and indicated with a beckoning hand to Giorgio to come and put himself between her legs.

Giorgio, mesmerised by what he was seeing, stood up and undid his belt. As he moved towards her, Janice licked her fingers and wetted herself and spread her legs in preparation for his cock. In just moments, Giorgio had pushed his way into her wet cunt as she let out a satisfied moan.

Then Janice put her hand over towards Alberto, discovered he had already let his member out, clasped hold of it, and sighed.

"Rallenta, rallenta," Janice called out in her limited Italian. She wanted Giorgio to slow down. She wanted a good and proper shagging that could go on for hours.

Alberto was wanting to do something with his cock. He was enjoying Janice's hand, but was intent on finding other parts of her body. Without losing Giorgio, Janice lifted herself and slid across onto Alberto, and before he knew it, was rubbing his cock against her willing anus.

"Culo! Culo!"

Moments later Alberto was in Janice's bottom, pushing upward as Giorgio pushed down. This was what Janice lived for and she groaned as her body sang and moved rhythmically on the two attentive cocks.

When Janice had enjoyed a long session with the men working for her in unison, she issued another instruction.

"Spingi più forte! Spingi più forte!" It worked, and both men pushed into her harder than ever.

They had been fucking Janice energetically for quite some time when she pushed both of them away and rolled over onto her knees.

"Cambiare!"

Janice was now poised with her cunt hovering above Alberto's solid member. Giorgio's throbbing penis waved from side to side and lifted itself up and down like a drawbridge, readying itself for Janice's backside. Janice's Italian language had worked and the two men had changed places. Alberto pushed his cock up into her just as Giorgio found the already open slippery orifice in Janice's rear. Janice crouched, fully impaled, staring into space and feeling those wonderful things which she mysteriously craved each day.

Finally both men, unable to withhold any longer, came in unison, filling her with cum in pulsating explosions. Satiated, Janice stood up and, without a word or a sign, picked up her panties and her frock and walked off into the shadowy garden, heading down to her car at the bottom of the drive.

As she got closer to the gate Janice noticed a couple in the moonlight, making love on the grass.

Without thinking, she walked over to them, knelt down and put her hand between their crotches, and took hold of the base of the man's shaft.

Janice removed it from the woman and put her head down and energetically licked the woman's cunt, thrusting her tongue in and eagerly biting a hard little clit as she savoured the flavours. Then she licked the man's cock, nibbling the end of it before she slipped it back in and stood up.

"Thanks," Janice murmured in her faraway voice as she walked away.

"Our pleasure!" came a woman's slurred voice. "Any time, darling."

Janice spread a hand towel on the driver's seat, knowing that she would be wet on the way home. There was only one thing left to do now and that was to get home and make a cup of cocoa, get into a bath, and then go to bed. Tomorrow was her therapy day. Her sister paid for it, but only on condition that Janice never missed a session.

Janice loved her therapist's voice. Benjamin Bauer's Viennese accent and soft vowels excited her beyond belief, and Janice loved the fact that he refused to fuck her. He asked only that she pull her skirt up high and stretch her long legs out and far apart, and touch herself while he watched her as he played with his cock and then masturbated.

That was enough for Janice, but only as long as Mr Bauer kept on talking. Sometimes he ran out of things to say while stroking himself; then he would panic and repeat things he had already said. He knew that if he stopped talking, his sexual fantasy would end. Janice would simply get up and leave.

Janice lay in her bath holding her mug of cocoa and not thinking about very much.

Then she remembered the shoes. Oh yes, she must wear her special heels tomorrow. Benji's shoes, she called them. Styled in Europe and worn by fancy ladies. She was certain that they kept Mr Bauer talking for much longer, and she liked that very much.

Fini

CATCH UP

EROS CRESCENT

No one on Eros Crescent remembers exactly the moment when the words COVID-19 or Corona virus were first uttered in their houses. Needless to say, it would first have been heard on a television report and the importance of the message would have taken a few days to sink in.

The world suddenly changed. Words and phrases like lockdown and self-isolation and social distancing were suddenly in the forefront of all conversations as people enacted the requests of government and the nation to act responsibly to assist in the national objective to achieve what quickly became known as flattening the curve.

For Roger, life couldn't have been less affected. His daily routines required only that he rose from his bed, showered and shaved, ate his breakfast, went for a walk, and made sure he had sufficient pens and paper. Although it did impinge on his new paying project.

He had been asked by Desley to write another booklet similar to the one he'd written for The Club, only this was to be for The Dunk-ing, a venue he had not yet visited or, until now, even heard of.

When Desley explained the concept and related what the setting inside the warehouse was like, Roger was very keen to get started. But the arrival of the virus put an end to that project, at least until further notice.

For Caroline and Jackie and Miranda, staying at home was what they enjoyed anyway, that is when they weren't travelling abroad or window shopping or having coffee in cafe's.

All three women had worked in executive positions in London, but moving overseas brought that era to a close, although they had been invited to join similar companies in Australia.

A top of the range coffee making machine was promptly ordered along with a supply of fair trade East Timorese Maubisse, medium blend. Browsing online shops became the new window shopping.

Instagram took on a new importance as the pandemic took hold around the world. Stories and pictures of people in isolation doing amazing and sometime ridiculous things became the rage. Jackie uploaded hundreds of images of the inside and outside of the house, earning the praise of interior designers and architects.

Helen and her husband Frederico were effected in so far as Freddy's job as a flight controller at the airport was soon to be reduced in the number of hours he worked. However, there was no threat to his income as he was on standby as an essential service. But Helen's work as a freelance Human Resources consultant to industry came to a sudden halt. She embraced online conferencing on Zoom but this was no substitute for real hands-on consulting.

Helen was also restricted in her love life, already reduced as a result of her husbands responsibilities to Helen's two lovers who had inadver-tently become pregnant to him.

Sophie and Freya now spent a night a fortnight with Freddy. Unable to visit or have visits from her own lovers, Polly or Celia Ashbee, Helen would just have to manage with her next-door neighbour, Mary. And what looked like the answer to maiden's prayer, The Club had been forced to close.

Mary's only loss of employment was her volunteer job at the Salvation Army Opportunity Shop which she would miss very much. She would also miss her sensual workout with her close friend Janice. But most of all, she would miss her newly found excitement at The Club which she had only recently opened.

Her niece and housemate, Sophie, worked at a horse stud and accepted reduced hours and looked forward to doing baby things at home. Because she and Mary lived next door to Helen and Freddy, the two households would have access to each other when needed. And of course, Freddy was to be the father of Sophie's as yet unborn child.

Alice and Frey both lamented the loss of work in their jobs as school counsellors. They both loved their jobs. Both were pregnant and accepted they would be forced to spend more time at home together.

Like most of the others, they had their favourite sex toys for when they weren't knitting baby clothes or doing jigsaw puzzles. And like so many women in lockdown, they visited female friendly porn sites online. The two decided that they would always share these internet session and happily parked themselves on the sofa, transmitting the websites from their phones to the giant television set via a magic little box. This meant that the images were so big that they felt they were in the same room and this proved most enjoyable on many occasions.

Bertie and Rosa were the older folk who were most vulnerable to the virus. They were happy to be isolated although Bertie complained that he would miss his fortnightly get together for coffee and cake with Freddy and Roger.

Bertie complained that he still had much to say on the subject of breaking down the worlds dependance on the "couples model" as he called it.

"Nothing good will happen while we maintain this ridiculous habit of pairing off for life. Firstly, in over half the cases, it doesn't work and people separated or divorced.

"Secondly, it was obvious that people who stayed in these relationships were deeply frustrated by the repressive demands on them of constantly answering to another person.

"Thirdly, paternity and property ownership where the only reasons this system was maintained and with the likely end of democracy as we know it looming, house prices and pension funds and equity investments were likely to collapse.

"And I haven't even mentioned the problems of religion and religious wars."

Rosa looked at him. She loved him dearly but managed always to call him out.

"You haven't mentioned love once."

"Sex and love are two seperate things, my dear. We both know that."

Most of the close friends and relatives knew that Rosa and Bertie had broken up many years ago and taken lovers. Rosa entered relationships with her close girl friends and occasionally, a man.

Sometime later, she and Bertie got back together as a couple, but both maintained their freedom to embark on other relationships if they so chose, and this arrangement worked very well. It wasn't that they were desperate to take on other romantic adventures, but just knowing that they were free to do so, made the difference. They broke up after almost twenty years and had now been together for nearly fifty years.

"It was a necessary pause," agreed the two of them, lovingly.

The two people that were originally going to be living together but in the end chose not too, were Edith and Jessica. But living at different ends of the same street meant that they would not need to forego their times together. And they, like Maude and the others living in number nineteen, had each other for company if and whenever they wanted.

Edith and Jessica had the boys on hand and could also still get a pizza delivered, although it sometimes took a little longer.

But then they learnt that they would now be sharing the boys with the very sexually active Maude and possibly with the two new girls who moved in to number eleven just before the lock down. Jessica and Edith's plans to invite the new girls in for a pizza, were in hand.

Edith still went for her walk on Mount Eros on most mornings where she usually met her friend Chloe and the two, more than not, would spend loving time together in Chloe's secret cave.

It was thanks to the lockdown, that Jessica met Chloe. Edith had long wanted the two to meet so when Jessica was unable to attend classes, she accompanied Edith on her walks.

Jessica and Chloe were instantly friends. Both knew that the other understood Chloe's relationship with Edith. And when the rain fortuitously arrived on their first walk together, all three made haste to the hidden cave and it was only a few minutes before Jessica had Chloe underneath her on the carpet of leaves with Edith dragging first Jessica's then Chloe's shorts and panties off before sitting beside them with her bare breasts available for the occasional grope from both girls.

It was Desley who had the most to lose but she wasn't particularly put out. The Club had to close only two short months after opening and only a few weeks after Desley had formed a partnership with her friend Sally who had opened The Dunking venue. The Dunking was closed too.

Desley welcomed the opportunity to take a rest and review everything about the club and the new venture and be ready to make any necessary changes or recommendations to Sally when they eventually reopened.

She and her partner Alvie, lived on the premises. Alvie knew about Desley's dalliances with Roger who she said she also had a soft spot for.

Desley had laughed, saying that now that they had so much time on their hands, she would endeavour to entice Roger to pop in for a threesome if Alvie didn't mind sharing. To which Alvie replied that she wanted first go.

Maria and her daughter Serina were at first, forced to stay home with grandfather Aldo and the boarder, Giorgio. They mostly worked for older people as cooks and housekeepers in the stately home of Vaucluse and Woollahra.

They successfully applied for positions with the council as carers so that they could continue working.

They both had each other and the two live-in men to play with when they felt like it plus a range of toys they enjoyed.

Maud, the owner of the music school and owner of the property at nineteen Eros Crescent found isolation difficult, severely limiting her adventures although she had managed to entertain herself with young Ashton and Damian after the two became suddenly sexually aware after falling prey to pizza nights with Jessica and Edith.

And Sylvia and Stella, the two girl who she had enjoyed briefly when they stayed over on the night of her house warming party, seducing Maude with the help their bunny outfits, had booked in for music classes and accomodation the week before lockdown. Maud reasoned that maybe life wouldn't be too bad after all.

Peoples attitudes were changed in part by the arrival of the pandemic.

Australia was fortunate that it could close its borders and clamp down easily on travel.

Europe was badly affected and Britain failed in the early stages to take action which might have prevented many of the casualties they suffered.

The USA continued to be the sad case that it had slowly become.

Big enough to make loud noises but also it seemed, too big to be able to maintain good democratic government.

It was presided over by a man who couldn't cope with an enemy he couldn't see and he couldn't lash out at, or verbally deride.

The arrival of the invisible virus was to prove his undoing.

Life on Eros Crescent went on. The residents continued to love each other in many different ways and despite the sudden disruption of the pandemic, there was a feeling of optimism in the air.

Babies were on the way and new life called out for new ideas. And new ideas about how society worked were desperately needed.

Cross your sanitised fingers everyone, and hope.

EPILOGUE

IN A MATRIARCHAL STRUCTURE, such as exists in some tribes in South India, women have natural confidence in their own woman-hood. They know their importance and that they are different from men in a special way, and this does not imply any inferiority. They are able to assert their human existence and being in a natural way.

So writes Marie Louise Von Franz in her book, *The Feminine in Fairy Tales.*

One should acknowledging Lilith, known by some as the Queen of the Night and by others as the ancient bad girl.

Lilith was said to have been Adams first wife. She was not happy with him and left. Her reasons included him always making her lie underneath him when making love and also demanding her complete obedience.

Eve replaced her and later Lilith was often represented in art by the serpent. (*See the sculpture at the entrance of Notre Dame cathedral depicting Adam and Eve, and Lilith as a serpent.*)

CONTACT

Publisher or review enquiries should include your full name and details
in all correspondence.

Email Address:
countrynotebook@gmail.com

RICHARD LEE PUBLISHING

Erotic Fiction

The Eros Crescent trilogy in separate volumes:

The Fifi Code

ISBN - 978-0-909431-02-0

Eros Crescent

ISBN - 978-0-909431-05-1

Mount Eros

ISBN - 978-0-909431-08-2

Excerpts from the Eros Crescent series:

Janice: A sexual enigma

Jessica: A young woman's journey

Helen: Enough is not enough

Maria: Always available

Mary: Catching Up

The Club: Ladies love it!

Literary Fiction

Australian Short Stories

ISBN - 978-0-909431-00-6

Restless: A novel about two young men growing up
in Australia between 1900 and 1936 (Publication date not set.)

Out of Print Titles

Mathematics for Young Children by Helen Western

ISBN - 978-0-909431-01-3

Currajong: For Those Whom Schools Have Failed

by Bruce Wicking

ISBN - 978-0-909431-03-7

The Puppetry Handbook by Anita Sinclair

ISBN - 978-0-909431-04-4

Wordswork by Chris Davidson & Bruce Wicking

ISBN - 978-0-909431-06-8

Sheep Production by Murray Elliott

ISBN - 978-0-909431-07-5

Ducks for Starters: A Practical Guide to

Backyard Duck Keeping by Bruce Wicking

ISBN - 978-1-875207-00-8

Sweethearts by Colin Talbot

ISBN - 978-1-875207-02-2

www.ingramcontent.com/pod-product-compliance
Lightning Source LLC
Chambersburg PA
CBHW020636130626
46552CB00003B/1257